MY 1ST GRAPHIC NOVEL®

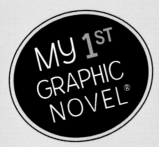

SHARK in the Library!

MY FIRST GRAPHIC NOVELS ARE PUBLISHED BY STONE ARCH BOOKS
A CAPSTONE IMPRINT
151 GOOD COUNSEL DRIVE, P.O. BOX 669
MANKATO, MINNESOTA 56002
WWW.CAPSTONEPUB.COM

Library of Congress Cataloging-in-Publication data is available on the
Library of Congress website.

ISBN: 978-1-4342-2058-5 (library binding)
ISBN: 978-1-4342-3104-8 (paperback)

Summary: Noah is thrilled when the week's library theme is sea creatures.
But when Noah can't find the stuffed shark, he is disappointed. Noah knows
there is a shark in the library, and he is going to find it!

Art Director: BOB LENTZ
Graphic Designer: EMILY HARRIS
Production Specialist: MICHELLE BIEDSCHEID

SHARK
in the
Library!

by Cari Meister
illustrated by Rémy Simard

STONE ARCH BOOKS
a capstone imprint

How To Read
A GRAPHIC NOVEL

Graphic novels are easy to read. Boxes called panels show you how to follow the story. Look at the panels from left to right and top to bottom.

Read the word boxes and word balloons from left to right as well. Don't forget the sound and action words in the pictures.

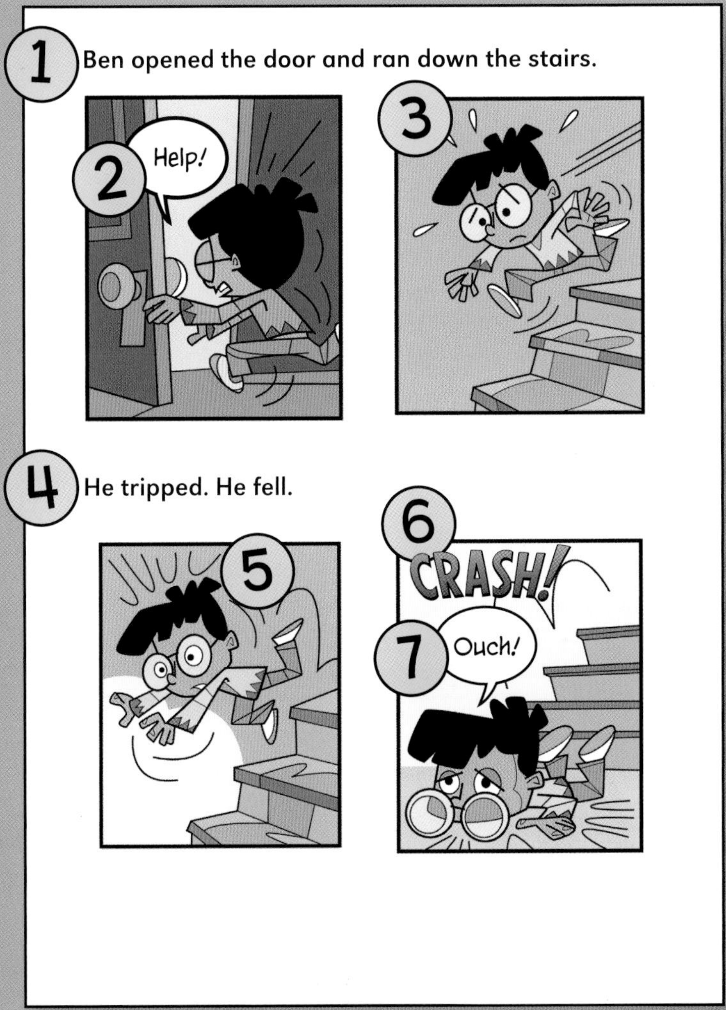
1
Ben opened the door and ran down the stairs.
2
Help!
3
4
He tripped. He fell.
5
6
CRASH!
7
Ouch!

The pictures and the words work together to tell the whole story.

It's library day for Noah's class. Library day only happens once a week.

Mrs. Brown greets the students. She is the librarian.

Every week, Mrs. Brown plans a new theme.
Last week was space week.

This week is sea creature week. There are sea
creatures everywhere!

Noah's class sits in a circle.

Mrs. Brown reads a funny story.

After the story, Mrs. Brown pulls out a big basket.

Mrs. Brown sticks one of the fish to the board.

Then she passes the basket around.

Ellie takes a baby seal.

Noah wants a shark, but he can't find one.

He takes a whale instead, but he isn't happy about it.

The class moves to the computers. They are going to research sea creatures.

Ellie types in "seal." Noah types in "shark."

Next, Mrs. Brown shows them where to find sea creature books. She shows them fiction and nonfiction books.

Noah finds a nonfiction book about sharks.

Ellie finds a fiction book about seals.

It's time to read to the sea creatures.

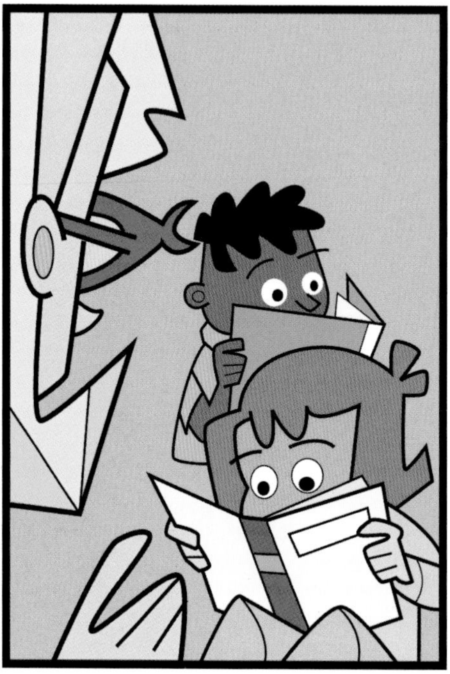

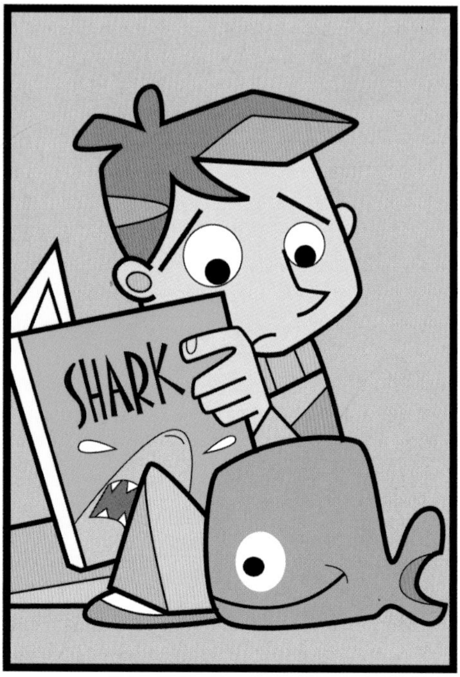
SHARK

When everyone is done reading, they put the books in the cart.

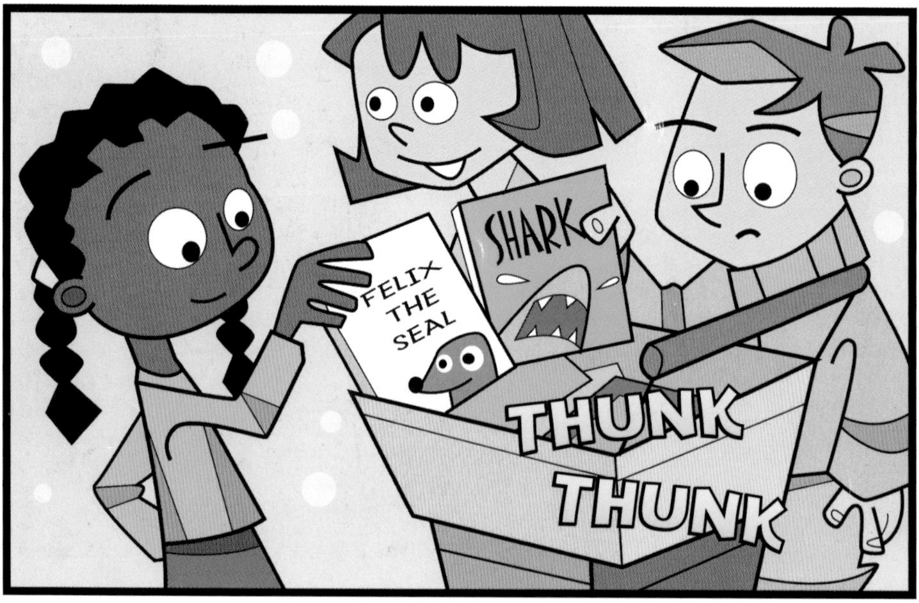
FELIX THE SEAL
SHARK
THUNK
THUNK

They put the sea creatures back in the basket for the next class.

Suddenly, Ellie starts jumping up and down and yelling.

I found the shark!

The shark is stuck to the back of
Noah's shirt.

Everyone laughs, including Mrs. Brown.

Mrs. Brown looks at the clock. The class only has five minutes left.

Ellie finds a book about sea plants. She also finds a puzzle.

Noah finds a book about killer whales.

He also finds a movie about sharks.

Noah's class lines up at the door.

Noah and Ellie leave the library with new books and big smiles.

The End

About the AUTHOR

Cari Meister is the author of many books for children, including the My Pony Jack series and *Luther's Halloween*. She lives on a small farm in Minnesota with her husband, four sons, three horses, one dog, and one cat. Cari enjoys running, snowshoeing, horseback riding, and yoga.

About the ILLUSTRATOR

Rémy Simard began his career as an illustrator in 1980. Today he creates computer-generated illustrations for a large variety of clients. He has also written and illustrated more than 30 children's books in both French and English, including *Monsieur Noir et Blanc*, a finalist for Canada's Governor's Prize. To relax, Rémy likes to race around on his motorcycle. Rémy resides in Montreal with his two sons and a cat named Billy.

GLOSSARY

FICTION (**FIK-shuhn**) — stories about characters and events that are not real

LIBRARY (**LYE-brer-ee**) — a place where books, magazines, newspapers, and more informational materials are kept

NONFICTION (**non-FIK-shuhn**) — stories about real events, people, and things

RESEARCH (**REE-surch**) — to study to find out about something

THEME (**THEEM**) — the main subject or idea

DISCUSSION QUESTIONS

1. The librarian picks a new theme every week. What theme would you pick? Why?

2. Do you like fiction or nonfiction books? Talk about your answer.

3. What is your favorite book? Why?

WRITING PROMPTS

1. Make your own book. Write a story and draw pictures to match.

2. Write a book report about this book. Be sure to include the setting, the characters, the main event, the problem, the conclusion, and if you liked or disliked the book.

3. Would you want to be a librarian? Write a paragraph explaining your answer.

The First Step into GRAPHIC NOVELS

These books are the perfect introduction to the world of safe, appealing graphic novels. Each story uses familiar topics, repeating patterns, and core vocabulary words appropriate for a beginning reader. Combine the entertaining story with comic book panels, exciting action elements, and bright colors and a safe graphic novel is born.

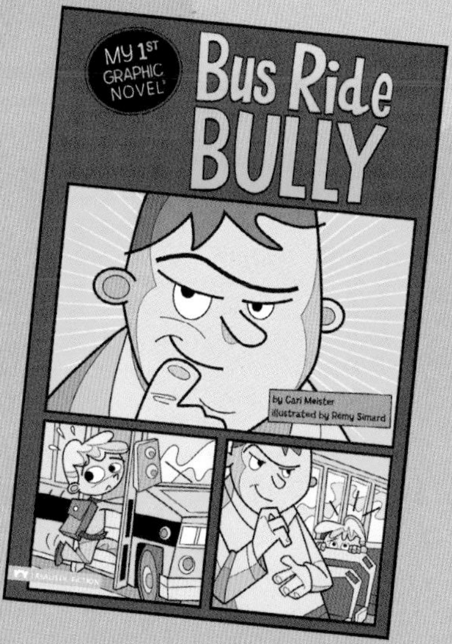
MY 1ST GRAPHIC NOVEL
Bus Ride BULLY
by Cari Meister
illustrated by Rémy Simard
REALISTIC FICTION

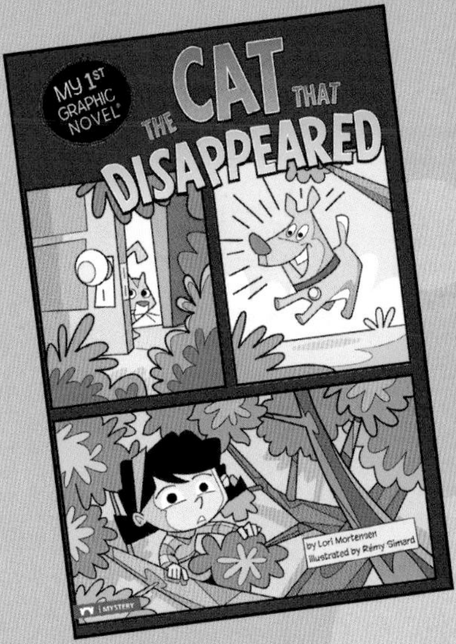
MY 1ST GRAPHIC NOVEL
THE CAT THAT DISAPPEARED
by Lori Mortensen
illustrated by Rémy Simard
MYSTERY

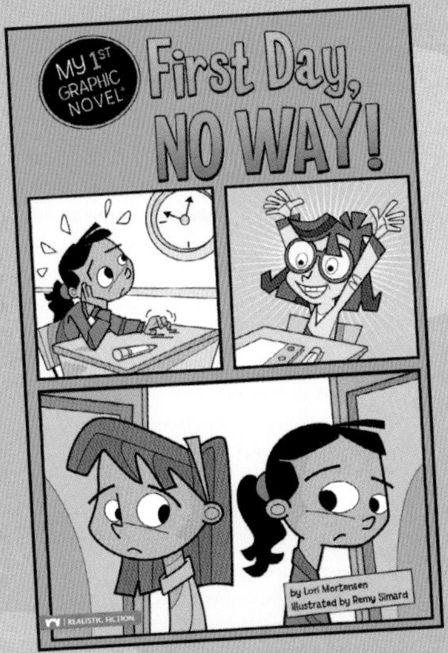
MY 1ST GRAPHIC NOVEL
First Day, NO WAY!
by Lori Mortensen
illustrated by Rémy Simard
REALISTIC FICTION

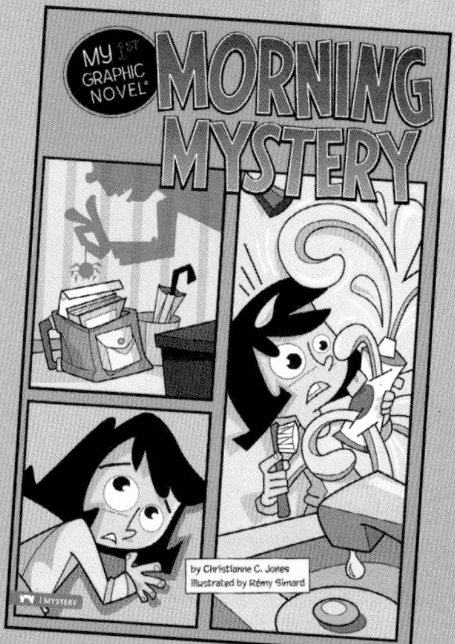
GRAPHIC NOVEL
MORNING MYSTERY
by Christianne C. Jones
illustrated by Rémy Simard
MYSTERY

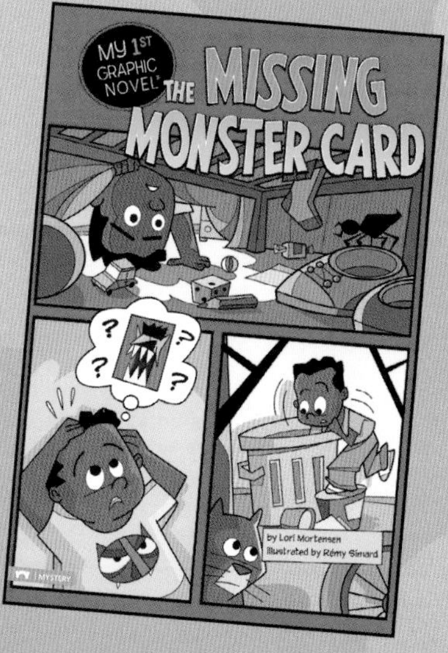
MY 1ST GRAPHIC NOVEL
THE MISSING MONSTER CARD
by Lori Mortensen
illustrated by Rémy Simard
MYSTERY

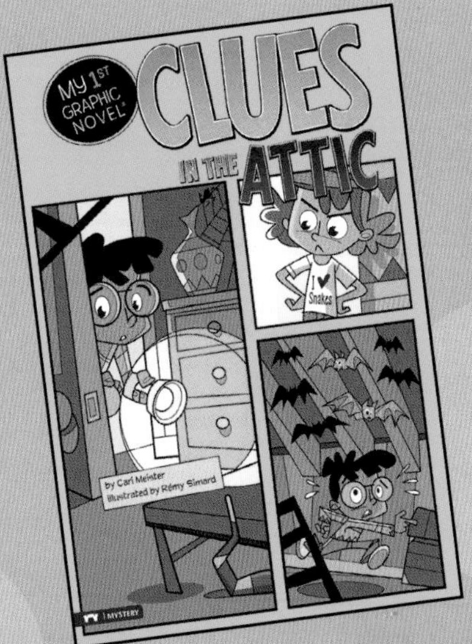
MY 1ST GRAPHIC NOVEL
CLUES IN THE ATTIC
I ♥ Snakes
by Cari Meister
illustrated by Rémy Simard
MYSTERY